Happily Ever After

Beauty and the Beast

To the man who became my prince.
Happily ever after.

First published in the UK in 2017
by New Frontier Publishing Pty Ltd
93 Harbord Street, London SW6 6PN
www.newfrontierpublishing.co.uk

ISBN: 978-0-9956255-4-9 (PB)

A CIP catalogue record for this book is available from
the British Library.

Designed by Celeste Hulme

Printed in China
10 9 8 7 6 5 4 3 2 1

Happily Ever After

Beauty and the Beast

Illustrated by Helene Magisson

There was once a rich merchant who had six children: three sons and three daughters. His youngest daughter Belle was called 'Beauty'. Everyone admired her.

The two eldest daughters went out to parties every night. They laughed at Beauty when she stayed at home to read books.

Suddenly the merchant became poor. His family had to move to the country. Beauty woke early every morning to clean the house and cook for the family. Her elder sisters did nothing.

When the merchant heard that a shipment of his goods was arriving in town he began to prepare for his journey. The family would soon be rich enough to move back to town. The eldest daughters asked their father to bring them back some new clothes. Beauty only asked for a rose.

When the merchant arrived to see his shipment he discovered there were no goods for him. He began his journey back home, still poor. As he walked through the forest he came upon an empty palace. He fed his hungry horse there and warmed himself by the fire.

The next morning he found a suit of clothes on his bed and a mug of hot chocolate waiting for him on the dining table.

Outside the snow had melted and in its place grew a beautiful garden full of roses. He went out to pick one for Beauty.

When the merchant had the rose in his hand he heard a terrible roar from across the garden.

'I have saved your life and in return you steal my roses?' bellowed the voice.

The merchant fell to his knees and looked up to see a horrible beast.

'I'm sorry,' he said, trembling with fear.

'I will forgive you,' said the Beast, 'as long as you send me one of your daughters.'

The merchant promised the Beast that he would.

'In your room is a chest,' said the Beast. 'Fill it with all the gold you can find in the palace. I will have it taken to your home.'

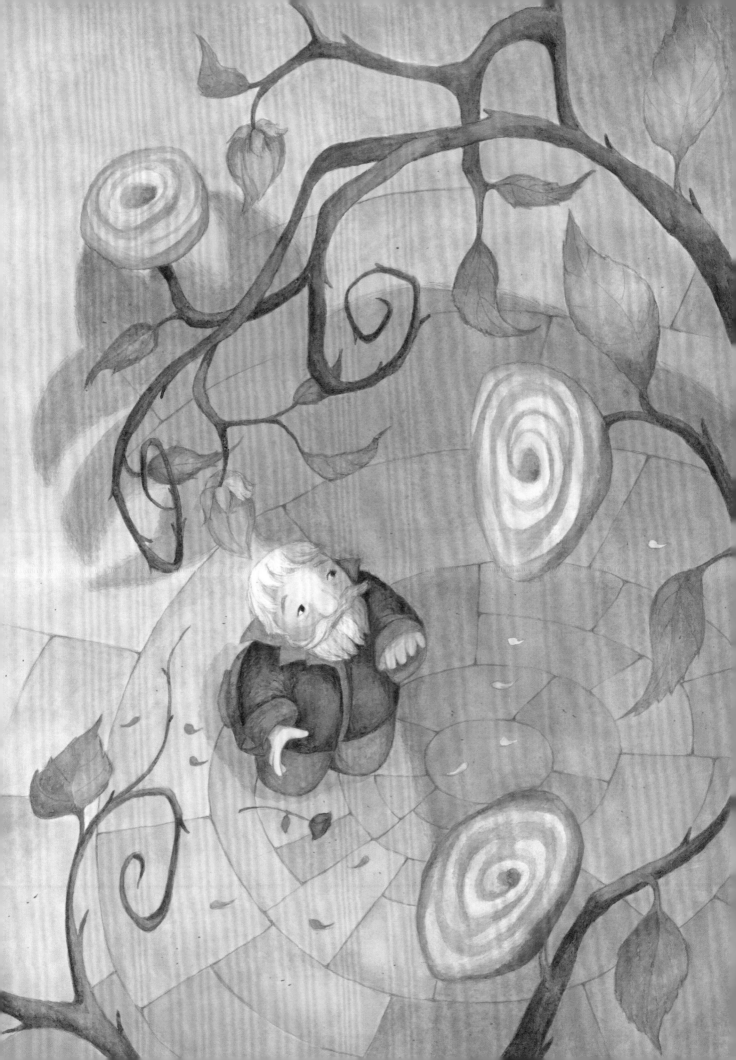

When the merchant returned home he was pale with the news.

'I will go, Father,' said Beauty. 'I was the one who wanted the rose.' Her father refused to allow it but Beauty insisted. She did not want her father to be punished.

Beauty and her father made their way to the palace. Beauty was frightened when she saw the Beast.

'Do you come willingly?' the Beast roared.

'Yes,' Beauty replied, shaking with fear.

With tears in his eyes the merchant left his daughter behind.

The next day Beauty walked alone through the Beast's castle. She discovered a door with her name on it: *Beauty's Room*. Inside the room was a magnificent library. She read the words inside the first book she opened.

Speak your wishes, it said.

'I want to see my father,' said Beauty.

As she spoke the words she saw her father appear in the mirror. He was returning home from his journey and at his feet was a chest full of gold. Then everything disappeared.

That evening dinner appeared for Beauty in the dining room. Out of the shadows stepped the Beast.

'Do you mind if I join you?' asked the Beast. 'I know I am ugly but I have a good heart.' Beauty was scared but agreed to let him sit with her.

When she had finished eating the Beast asked, 'Will you marry me?'

'No, Beast,' answered Beauty.

The Beast let out a roar that echoed around the palace. He stood up and walked away.